PUFFIN BOOKS

MRS COCKLE'S CAT

Old Mrs Cockle and her cat Peter live very happily at the top of their London house. Mrs Cockle is very fond of Peter, _____ _____ _____ else, and he in his turn is very _____ _____ _____ thing that he loves more than _____ Cockle and _____ fresh fish for his supper. One summer, when the weather is bad, the fishermen can't take their boats out to sea and so poor Peter has to go without. But he soon decides to do something about the terrible fishless situation and runs away in search of his favourite food. Poor Mrs Cockle pines for his company and grows so thin that a puff of wind could have blown her away, as the saying goes. And a puff of wind does . . .

Philippa Pearce was born and brought up in the Cambridgeshire village where she now lives. For a time she lived in London, where she worked as a scriptwriter and producer in radio, for the School Broadcasting service of the BBC, and then as the children's editor of André Deutsch Ltd. Her novels for older children include *Tom's Midnight Garden*, which was awarded the Carnegie Medal in 1958, and, for younger children, *The Battle of Bubble and Squeak*, winner of the Whitbread Award.

PHILIPPA PEARCE

Mrs Cockle's Cat

WITH DRAWINGS BY ANTONY MAITLAND

PUFFIN BOOKS

PUFFIN BOOKS

Published by the Penguin Group
Penguin Books Ltd, 27 Wrights Lane, London W8 5TZ, England
Penguin Books USA Inc., 375 Hudson Street, New York, New York 10014, USA
Penguin Books Australia Ltd, Ringwood, Victoria, Australia
Penguin Books Canada Ltd, 10 Alcorn Avenue, Toronto, Ontario, Canada M4V 3B2
Penguin Books (NZ) Ltd, 182–190 Wairau Road, Auckland 10, New Zealand

Penguin Books Ltd, Registered Offices: Harmondsworth, Middlesex, England

This edition first published by Viking Kestrel 1987
Published in Puffin Books 1988
5 7 9 10 8 6 4

Text copyright © Philippa Pearce, 1961
Illustrations copyright © Antony Maitland, 1987
All rights reserved

Printed in England by Clays Ltd, St Ives plc
Filmset in Baskerville (Linotron 202)

Old Mrs Cockle lived at the top of a
very tall house in London. Most of the
people who knew her were sorry for
her, because she had to climb eighty-
four stairs before she reached her own
front-door; but she did not mind. It is
true that all that climbing made the
backs of her knees ache, but then there

were advantages. Mrs Cockle lived so
high that, from her window, she had a
view of the sky over the top of the tall
house opposite – which was more than

most people had. In the mornings she could look out and think, The sky is blue all over – I'll wear my straw bonnet today; or, The sky is white with snow coming – I'll wear my woollen shawl today; or, The sky has clouded right over – I'll take my biggest umbrella. Mrs Cockle had three umbrellas for different weathers, and the biggest of the three was larger than umbrellas are ever made nowadays.

There was another advantage for Mrs Cockle in living at the very top of the house. In the middle of her ceiling there was a trapdoor, and, if she set up her step-ladder underneath it, she could climb up, open the trapdoor, and climb through on to the roof itself.

From the roof she could look round
over the buildings of London, and see
the factory chimneys and church-
spires, and, more than anything else,
the chimney-pots – more chimney-pots
than you could ever have counted –
rows upon rows of chimney-pots that
seemed to melt away into the smoky
distances of London.

This was a fine view, but Mrs

Cockle, with the backs of her knees
already aching from the eighty-four
stairs, would never have bothered
about the roof but for Peter. Peter, who
was a cat and lived with Mrs Cockle,
was very fond of the roof on a sunny
day, or sometimes at night when the
moon was full. It was one of the three
things that Peter Cockle loved most.

The other two things were a little fresh fish for his tea and Mrs Cockle's company. Mrs Cockle, in her turn, was very fond of Peter – more fond of him than of anybody else, for she had no relations, and Mr Cockle had died long before.

Old Mrs Cockle and her cat lived together very contentedly. Every fine day, early, Mrs Cockle opened the trapdoor for Peter to climb on to the roof. Then she set out for her day's work, which was selling coloured balloons at the corner of one of the great London streets. There are plenty of people who sell balloons at street corners in the summer-time or at Christmas; Mrs Cockle was the only person in London who could be counted upon to be selling balloons at

her corner, all the year round, day in,
day out, and whatever the weather.
And, as she said, she did just
comfortably enough out of it for herself
and Peter.

Late one summer the weather had been particularly wet and blowy, without making any difference to Mrs Cockle; but it had made a difference to Peter. In the first place, he had not cared to venture out on to the roof as usual: that meant that he missed his fresh air and exercise, and felt stuffy and cross, as people do. Besides, he really had something to be cross about. The weather was so bad that the fishermen could not put out to sea as often as usual; there was less fish

caught and taken to London and so
what little there was in the shops was
very dear – too dear for Mrs Cockle to
buy. Instead of having fresh fish for his
tea every day, Peter had to put up with
now a saucer of milk, now some dried
haddock, now milk again, now half a
tin of herrings in tomato sauce, and so
on.

Peter Cockle longed and longed for a
mouthful of fresh fish. He knew at last
that he loved fresh fish more than a
breath of air on the roof, and more
even than Mrs Cockle's company. In

his own mind, he even blamed Mrs
Cockle for the lack of fresh fish,
although it was hardly her fault.
Nowadays, in the evening, when he

and Mrs Cockle sat on either side of
the fire with the high wind outside
rattling at the windows, they were not
as cosy as they used to be. Mrs Cockle
sat rocking herself, and knitting, and
glancing fondly at Peter. But Peter had
given up looking back at her at all: he
gazed moodily into the flames of the
fire, and saw there nothing but the
glittering, slithering shapes of Fresh
Fish. And while Mrs Cockle was
thinking proudly what a handsome cat
he was, Peter was thinking deeply of
Fresh Fish until his head seemed to
swim with them. And when Mrs
Cockle dozed off, Peter was kept awake
by the remembrance of Fresh Fish that
seemed to be felt now in his stomach,
now on his tongue, and now between
his paws.

It was not only in the long quiet
evenings that Peter Cockle suffered.
One night he could not get to sleep at
all for thinking of Fresh Fish. It was
then that he took his resolution. Next
morning, instead of either mewing to
be let out on to the roof, or staying
curled up on his cushion, he was falsely
purring around Mrs Cockle's ankles as
she prepared to set out. When she went
to the door, he was already there,
waiting to say goodbye. But when she

opened the door he was out of it ahead of her, and, like a black streak, leaping down the eighty-four steps to the street below.

'Peter! Peter!' called Mrs Cockle distractedly, but there was no sign of his coming back. She climbed down the stairs, hoping to find him waiting for her out in the street. Outside, there was not a cat in sight, except the tabby from next door, and he disliked Mrs Cockle and would not show by as much as a quiver of a whisker which way he had seen Peter go.

'Peter! Peter!' called Mrs Cockle, but softly, because she did not want to start the neighbours talking. No cat came.

Mrs Cockle was naturally upset, but there was nothing to be done, so she went off to her street-corner as usual. She said to herself that the wilful cat would certainly be waiting outside the front door when she went home in the evening. She was only worried about what might happen to him in the

meantime. Just suppose, Mrs Cockle
thought, he tried to sneak a piece of
nice fresh fish from somebody's larder,
and they set a dog after him? Or worse,
supposing he tried to steal something
from the fish shop, and a policeman
caught him at it?

That evening Mrs Cockle hurried home a little earlier than usual. There was no Peter in the street outside, and the tabby cat seemed to be sneering. She paid no attention, but hurried up the eighty-four stairs, hoping that, in spite of the tabby cat's expression, Peter might be waiting at the top. But at the very top, there was still no Peter, and poor Mrs Cockle suddenly felt, for

the first time in her life, that eighty-
four stairs had been too much for her.
She sat down on the top one and cried.

There was no Peter Cockle that day,
nor the next, nor the next. Mrs Cockle
tried to go on as usual without him –
going to her street-corner, selling
balloons, coming home to supper, and
going to bed. But her day did not seem
the same without a cat: she could not
eat properly at mealtimes, nor sleep
properly at nights. As time went by she
grew thinner and thinner from worry
and lack of sleep and lack of food. At
last, from being the plumpest balloon-
seller in London, she became – so
many believed – by far the thinnest.
She looked as thin and light as an
autumn leaf as she hurried to work
along the windy pavements.

One morning, many weeks after
Peter's disappearance, Mrs Cockle
saw from the sky that the day was
going to be wet and very blowy. She
put on her goloshes to keep her feet
dry, took the largest of her three
umbrellas to keep the rest of her dry,
and set out to work. It was not yet
raining, although the clouds were thick
and low overhead; but the wind was

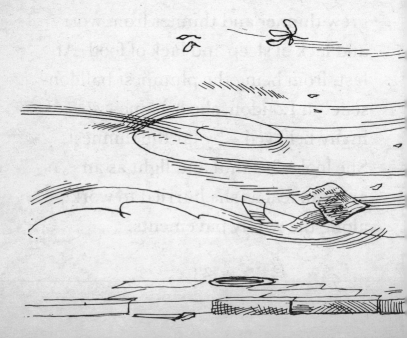

already blowing so strongly that she took much longer than usual to reach her street-corner. The hour was still very early and there was no one about. Mrs Cockle hooked her umbrella, still unopened, over her arm, and began blowing up her balloons. Each one, when she had blown it up, she tied for the time being to the iron-fencing. When she had blown them all up – and

she had brought out more balloons than usual that morning – she untied them, one by one, to hold them all together in her hand, ready for selling.

At the instant that Mrs Cockle grasped all the balloons in her hand, a great gust of wind came round the corner. It tugged hard at the bunch of balloons, and almost lifted her off her feet, so that she thought she was going to topple over. Instead of falling, however, she felt herself rising. Mrs Cockle's extra thinness and lightness, which had come since Peter's disappearance, and the extra number of balloons that morning, and the extra strong wind at that instant, all helped to lift the old woman clean off her feet, and she began floating upwards. She was so taken by surprise that, for the

first few feet upwards, she did not think
of calling for help; and after that she
felt, as she said later, that she hardly
wished to call attention to her position.

Luckily she kept a tight hold on her great bunch of balloons, so that there was no danger of a sudden fall. Even the big umbrella still hung safely from the crook of her arm.

Mrs Cockle went steadily up. She floated up past the first-floor windows of the houses, and saw a young man in pyjamas shaving. She floated past the second-floor windows, and saw two little girls making their beds. Past the third-floor windows, where she saw a

whole family sitting down to a
breakfast of sausages and bacon. Past
the fourth-floor windows, where a fat
gentleman was doing exercises to keep
down his waist measurements. And,
lastly, past the attics on the fifth floor,
where she saw a boy in bed with
measles. He was the only person who

saw, first of all, the great bunch of red and blue and yellow balloons, rising steadily, and then, dangling underneath them, Mrs Cockle. She rose into view and then rose out of it. The boy called his mother in to tell her, but she only thought he must be in a very high fever, and never believed a word.

The balloons and Mrs Cockle were now rising well above the highest of the houses – higher than she and Peter had ever been on their own roof-top. At first a wonderful view of all London appeared beneath her; but in another instant it vanished, and Mrs Cockle found herself mounting – much more slowly now – into a damp, dingy, foggy mist, which was really the heavy rain-cloud she had noticed earlier in the day.

The mist made her feel cold and damp and uncomfortable all over. It was so thick that Mrs Cockle was only rising through it extremely slowly. She began to wonder whether she was going to be the only balloon-seller in London to end her days in a rain-cloud.

Suddenly Mrs Cockle felt a pleasant
warmth on her knuckles where, above
her head, they grasped the strings of
her balloons. She looked up and saw a
radiance brightening through the
cloud. She was now rising a little faster,
and in a few moments she burst out of

the rain-cloud altogether. Now she saw
why her knuckles had felt warm and
why she had seen a brightness: on the
other side of the thick clouds the sun
was shining warmly and brightly, as on
a summer's day. Overhead the sky was
a speckless blue, and beneath Mrs
Cockle's feet the rain-cloud itself, with
the sunshine upon it, now looked as
white and gleaming as a snowfield.
Mrs Cockle thought it looked rather
like the top of her own wedding-cake
all those years ago – and there was
certainly an air of celebration about
the glittering scene.

Beneath the clouds, London must be cold and wet and windy, but here the weather was perfect. There was hardly more than a breeze, so that Mrs Cockle's balloons were not tempted to float her up any higher. Instead, they gave her just enough support for her to be able to walk, in a rather feathery, bouncy fashion, on the surface of the cloudland. The feeling of half walking, half floating along, as light as one of her own balloons, was so delightful that Mrs Cockle forgot all her troubles – forgot Peter even. She was a gay old

woman at heart, and she had the
common sense to realize that she was
unlikely ever to have such an
experience as this again. She practised
little runs and jumps that, without any
effort, carried her for yards at a time.
She looked round and admired the
changing cloud-scenery – the clouds
that moved lazily and puffed
themselves up into twisted, toppling
mountains, or swirled away to leave
mysterious caverns into which she
peered, or even drew away altogether
to leave gulfs and abysses.

It was while Mrs Cockle was peering over the edge of one of these gaps in the clouds that she suddenly realized how high up she was, and, for the first time, felt giddy. Far, far below were the roofs of London, and no way of getting safely down to them, that she could think of. She wished aloud that she were a cat, like Peter, with nine lives, for she would need them all to get safely to earth again. Then she wished that Peter were there with her, because cats are so resourceful. But, of course, wishing was no good.

Mrs Cockle was a sensible old woman, and resourceful, even without Peter. Through the gap in the clouds, she had caught a glimpse of the River Thames, and now she determined to keep above it as long as she could: she felt that her old bones would fall more softly into water – if fall they must – than on to hard chimney-pots. So she looked through any holes in the clouds

as often as she could, to keep the River Thames in sight, and from above she followed its dark, twisting course as far as she was able. She had to keep on the move, anyway, because, if she stood still, she at once began gently to sink through the cloud surface, and the damp of the mist would begin to come up over the tops of her goloshes.

In the ordinary way, for someone to walk along the River Thames from London down to the river's mouth

would be very long and dull and tiring.
For Mrs Cockle, tripping along lightly
overhead, it was none of these things.
Only towards the end did she even
begin to wish there were a cup of tea to
be had.

At last, after walking without effort
all morning and part of the afternoon,
Mrs Cockle came within sight of the
end of her cloudland. Really it was not
so much that the cloud came to an end,
as that it was now beginning to melt

away altogether. The bad weather of so
many weeks was changing, the clouds
were vanishing, and the day was going
to clear up. What interested Mrs
Cockle, more than the weather, was
what lay over the broken edge of the
clouds. Soon she saw: it was the sea.
She had followed the River Thames
from London down to its very mouth,
where it runs into the sea. She was over
the sea itself.

Her first feeling was of thankfulness that now, if the worst came to the worst, there were no chimney-pots at all to fall upon. Her next feeling was one of curiosity, for Mrs Cockle had never seen the sea – although she had, of course, heard about it. After all, you cannot have a reliable name for selling balloons in London every day in the year *and* be able to take a day off at the seaside. Besides, the train fare would have been more than Mrs Cockle could afford, if she were to keep Peter in the comfort to which he was accustomed. So this was the very first time Mrs Cockle had seen the sea; and she meant to make the most of it. Her prudence held her back from going too near the cloud edge, but all the same,

in her eagerness, she did not notice
that the cloud itself was steadily
melting away. Suddenly a hole came
under her right foot, which at once
sank through it; at the same time, a
wisp of cloud curling back on itself
tripped up her left foot, and in an
instant Mrs Cockle had fallen over the
edge.

In the confusion of losing her balance Mrs Cockle let go of the balloons, and they soared away into the highest air and were never seen again. For a few seconds after that, Mrs Cockle fell very rapidly; then her enormous umbrella, which had been jerked up without losing its hold on her arm, opened out of its own accord – as umbrellas will do, in such circumstances. Mrs Cockle clung tightly to it, and felt it steady her, as it opened above her like a parachute.

Now she was dropping through the
air quite gently, although fairly fast.
She dared to look down at the
wonderful strange sea below, and saw
it as she would never see it again — a

blue surface scrawled and scribbled over with little wavering lines of white that were foam. Below her, on the sea, was a black speck which, as she came lower, she could make out to be a fishing-boat. It was the first of the boats to put out to sea to take advantage of the better weather. The bottom of the boat was already silver with newly-caught fish, and the young fisherman was already hauling his nets in for the second time.

As she came lower, Mrs Cockle
called to the man in the boat, but
either he was too busy to hear her, or
else he could not believe a voice would
come from above him. The next
minute, Mrs Cockle's feet touched sea-
water for the first time in their life, and
in the next instant the whole of Mrs
Cockle was sinking into it. She could
not swim, and she had heard that the
sea could be very deep, so that she was
relieved but surprised to find

something solid – or nearly solid –
under her feet. Just then the young
fisherman, whose net she was feeling
beneath her, called out crossly: 'What
are you doing in my fishing net?'

Mrs Cockle would have begun to
answer his question but for something
very surprising – the really astounding
part of this story. This astounding
thing made Mrs Cockle call back,

'And, pray, what are you doing with that cat in your fishing-boat?' For there sat Peter Cockle.

He sat in the bows of the boat, paying no attention to men hauling in nets, or old women falling from the skies into them. He was staring steadily at the fresh fish that were piling up in the bottom of the boat. Although he had been too well brought

up by Mrs Cockle not to know how to
wait for his meals, the tip of his pink
tongue was caught between his teeth as
though it had positively to be kept back
from the feast.

Peter sat there, while the fisherman
hauled his nets in and helped Mrs
Cockle aboard and said he was sorry if
he had spoken roughly but it had all
been so unexpected. Mrs Cockle said
she was sorry too, and hoped she
hadn't done any harm to the nets but
she was always very light upon her

feet. Then the young man put his dry
jacket round Mrs Cockle's shoulders
and said he would row her back to land
at once, because he could see that what
she needed was a cup of hot tea. While
he rowed, Mrs Cockle asked him very
politely about the cat who sat so
quietly in the bows.

'Oh, him!' said the fisherman. 'He turned up a week or more ago, very thin and raggy-coated, and his foot-pads worn thin with walking from wherever he came from. All the same he looked a handsome cat, so many a one would have taken him in. The milkman tried to tempt him with a dish of cream, but he wouldn't go. Then the grocer tried him with potted shrimps:

he'd have none of them. Instead, he
spent his time hanging round the
fishing-boats and nets on the shore. In
the end, I believe he took a fancy to
me, and I'll tell you why I think it. I've
put to sea when other fishermen
daren't, and I've always fed him on a
little of the catch, however poor it was.
It's my belief, ma'am, that that cat is
partial to a bit of fresh fish.'

At the end of the fisherman's story, Peter caught Mrs Cockle's eye by mistake. It was no longer any use to pretend that he did not see her, so – looking very ashamed of himself – Peter stepped across and rubbed himself timidly against her goloshes. Mrs Cockle ought to have been very offended, but she loved Peter too dearly. She bent down and tickled him under the chin, at which Peter instantly began to purr. The young fisherman smiled; Mrs Cockle smiled; and Peter took courage and purred very loudly.

When they reached land, the
fisherman took Peter and Mrs Cockle
to the little hut where he lived all by

himself. There he made Mrs Cockle a cup of hot, strong tea. When she had finished, she asked the young man if it would be convenient for her to come and keep house for him, since she had taken such a strong fancy to his cat. He was a little surprised at first; but, on turning the idea over in his mind, he saw what an excellent one it was. So things were arranged.

Mrs Cockle settled down to her duties at once. In the mornings she got up very early, cleaned the little house, made the breakfast, packed a lunch for Peter and the fisherman, and said goodbye to them when they sailed away to fish. Then, if the fancy took her, she went about her old business of selling balloons, which she did now in a sheltered corner of the promenade. She liked the promenade better than her London street: she could see so much of the sky and the sea, and – better still – she could keep an eye on Peter, far out in the fishing-boat.

When she saw the boat coming back, she packed up her balloons and hurried home ahead of the other two, to get their tea ready. There was always a nice piece of fresh fish for

Peter's tea, and the young fisherman
used to reflect how thoughtful dear
Mrs Cockle was of his cat.

Mrs Cockle never told that Peter had once lived with her in London and then left her: she would not have had people think that Peter was light in his affections. She knew in her heart that, after fresh fish for his tea, Peter Cockle valued her company more than anything else in the world.

THE GIRAFFE AND THE PELLY AND ME

Roald Dahl/Quentin Blake

What else could a giraffe with an extending neck, a pelican with an expanding beak and an athletic little monkey be but The Ladderless Window-Cleaning Company? When this amazing trio are invited to try and clean all the 677 windows belonging to His Grace the Duke of Hampshire, it is no wonder that they have the most incredible adventures, with young Billy there to join in the fun.

CHRIS AND THE DRAGON

Fay Sampson

Chris is always in trouble of one kind or another but does try extra-hard to be good when he is chosen to play Joseph in the school Nativity play. A hilarious story, which ends with a glorious celebration of the Chinese New Year.

RADIO ALERT
RADIO DETECTIVE
RADIO REPORTERS
RADIO RESCUE
RADIO TRAP

John Escott

Five exciting stories centred on a local radio station, Round-bay Radio. In each story there's a mystery which the children involved help to solve brilliantly.